W9-BYU-555

# ARCTIC HUNTER

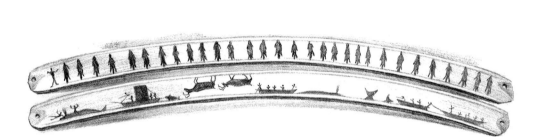

Text copyright ©1992 by Diane Hoyt-Goldsmith

Photographs copyright ©1992 by Lawrence Migdale

Aerial photograph copyright ©1990 by Tommy Ongtooguk

Text illustrations copyright ©1992 by Lloyd Goldsmith
    from a sketch of ivory sculpture and drill bows by Ludovik Choris,
    artist of Otto von Kotzebue's expedition to the Arctic in 1816.

Map copyright ©1992 by Mas Miyamoto

All rights reserved

Printed in the United States of America

First Edition

LIBRARY OF CONGRESS CATALOGING-IN-PUBLICATION DATA
Hoyt-Goldsmith, Diane.
    Arctic hunter / Diane Hoyt-Goldsmith; photographs by Lawrence Migdale.
            p.            cm.
    Summary: A ten-year-old Eskimo (Inupiat) boy who lives far north
of the Arctic Circle describes his family's annual spring trip to
their camp, where they spend several weeks hunting and fishing for
food to supplement their diet for the rest of the year and enjoying
old traditions.
    ISBN 0-8234-0972-4
    1. Eskimos–Alaska–Kotzebue–Hunting–Juvenile literature.
2. Eskimos–Alaska–Kotzebue–Social life and customs–Juvenile
literature.   3. Kotzebue (Alaska)–Social life and customs–Juvenile
literature.   [1. Eskimos.   2. Indians of North America.]
I. Migdale, Lawrence, ill. II. Title.
E99.E7H867    1992      92-2563     CIP       AC
979.8'7–dc20

ACKNOWLEDGMENTS
In creating this book, we enjoyed the enthusiasm and cooperation of many people.
We would like to give special thanks to the Joule family of Kotzebue, Alaska: to
Reggie and Linda, to their children LaVisa, Angela, Dawn, Puyuk, and especially
Reggie Jr. The Joule family, along with Ross and Millie Schaeffer, taught us many
things about the Arctic and the Iñupiaq way of life. They invited us to share some
unique and unforgettable experiences, and we are forever in their debt. We have
deep affection and respect for Vera Douglas, who shared her knowledge of
all things with such humor and pride, and we appreciate the enthusiasm of three
young friends, Johnson Goodwin, Eddie Kootuk, and Derrick Fox, who shared our
adventures on Sadie Creek.

    It would have been impossible to do this book without the support and
advice of special people like Judy Nõmmik, who helped us in our early research
and introduced us to the Joules. We also thank Linda Justine Ellana, Judith Greene,
Risa Keene, Laurie Pease, Scott Warren, and the Kotzebue Inupiat Dancers for their
help. Ruth Sampson of the Bilingual Program in Kotzebue was most helpful in
editing the text and giving advice about Iñupiaq translations.

    Lorna Mason and Mike Larkin have both contributed their special expertise
and have enriched this project with their efforts.

AUTHOR'S NOTE

Beginning with the passing of the Marine
Mammal Protection Act of 1972, there has been
steady growth in regulatory actions to control
and protect subsistence hunting. The laws support the non-commercial harvest of animals for
food and at the same time protect the animals
against abuses.

    In the formation of the National Parks sys-
tem in North Alaska, special recognition was
given to subsistence hunting, fishing and gath-
ering. These traditional activities are at the very
heart of the region's cultural character, and they
dominate land use discussions. Special preserves
have been created to allow for the continued
existence of hunting lifestyles. Thus the Inupiat
will continue to live, balancing their own needs
with those of the arctic environment.

# ARCTIC HUNTER

BY DIANE HOYT–GOLDSMITH

PHOTOGRAPHS BY LAWRENCE MIGDALE

HOLIDAY HOUSE • NEW YORK

Juv.
E99.E7 H867   1992

This book is dedicated to
Vera Douglas of Shungnak, Alaska,
and to the elders like her who keep alive
the ancient language and customs
of the Iñupiaq people

My name is Reggie. I live in Kotzebue (*COTS-eh-byoo*), Alaska, a town far to the north above the Arctic Circle. People believe that my ancestors came to this land many thousands of years ago, crossing the Bering Sea from Asia. Today some people call us Eskimos, but we call ourselves the Inupiat (*ee-nyoo-PAYT*). In our language this means "the real people." Our ancestors have taught us many ways to live in this land of ice and snow, of long winter nights and never-ending summer days.

For much of the year, the days are dark and cold. From October until June, ice and snow cover the ground. Because we live above the Arctic Circle, the sun peeks above the horizon for only a few hours a day. During many months of winter, these hours of twilight are all that separate one day from the next.

# BREAKUP
## SIKULIQIRUQ

Our town is on a peninsula at the edge of the Chukchi (*CHUHK-CHEE*) Sea. In winter, miles of ocean freeze over and the ice is locked hard against the shoreline. It seems that the dark and the cold will go on forever.

But gradually the days get longer. The position of the sun changes until the sun is always above the horizon, and it is never dark. Then spring and summer blend into one long day that lasts for months. The long hours of sunshine warm the air and a new drama begins.

In early June, we hear the sound of cracking, like a gunshot, as the ice on the shore begins to melt. As the days pass, we hear the loud booming more often as we go to school or lie in our beds at night.

After a few weeks, huge chunks of ice start to float free. Ocean currents carry the ice away from shore and out toward the open sea. Even the land, which has been covered with snow since autumn, shows through in patches of brown as the sun beats down.

This is a time we call breakup. When the great mass of ice floats away from our shores, we can travel on the ocean in our boats. As the snow melts on land, we can find the plants and berries that have been buried all winter.

Suddenly, there are many changes. When breakup comes, there is a lot of outdoor activity and excitement. Boats and kayaks come out of storage. People finish mending their fishnets and clean their rifles. Breakup signals the beginning of a special season for the Inupiat. We go to our camps in the wilderness to harvest the foods that we will need the next winter.

Every year my family travels to the same camp to hunt and fish. We leave right after breakup in early June and stay for several weeks. Our friends Ross and Millie always go to camp with us. Ross is a great hunter, and Millie teaches us about preserving all the foods we find. This year, we invited a few of my friends to come along too.

The camp is on the coast south of Kotzebue, at a place where a small river enters the sea. We call our camp Sadie (*SAY-dee*) Creek after the river.

In the spring, the solid sheets of ice begin to melt, crack, and break apart. Soon the masses of ice float away from the shoreline and the sea opens up to boat travel.

6

Reggie visits a supermarket in Kotzebue with his parents to buy food to take to camp. They buy bananas and apples, granola and peanut butter, and their favorite Sailor Boy crackers.

The night before leaving for camp, Reggie helps Vera tie wooden floats to the top of a fishnet. Vera lives many miles away in a small village on the Kobuk River called Shungnak (SHUN-nyack). Reggie and his sisters call her Aana (AH-nah), a term of respect that also means "grandmother" in their language. Vera will go to the camp at Sadie Creek with Reggie's family. She likes to teach the children about the traditional Iñupiaq (in-yoo-PAK) ways.

# GOING OUT TO CAMP
## AULLAAŁIQ

Getting to our camp is a real adventure. We never know what to expect. There are very few roads around Kotzebue and those we have are unpaved and full of potholes. It is hard to drive a car over them because they are so bumpy and muddy.

Like most people in Kotzebue, we have a four-wheel-drive truck. We load our truck with boxes of supplies and pile it high with gear. Then we set off down the coast. We drive as far as we can, but soon a large snowbank cuts off our travel. It stretches across the beach and into the sea, so we have to leave our truck behind.

From this point, we use our four-wheeler. About the size of a motorcycle, this all-terrain vehicle is used for rugged travel and pulls a small trailer behind it. Because we can drive it over snow, we use it to shuttle everything down the beach to the mouth of the river near camp. We all take turns riding and walking the last few miles of our journey.

On the way to camp, the family stops for a picnic lunch along the beach. Reggie and his friend Eddie build a driftwood fire for making hot tea.

When we finally arrive at Sadie Creek, the tide is in and the river crossing is flooded with six or seven feet of freezing water. We are not able to drive the four-wheeler across the shallows as we had planned. But our friend Ross, who has lived in the Arctic all his life, is not discouraged. He has a good idea.

He decides to snag an ice floe. Taking one of our long wooden tent poles, he jabs at a large piece of ice that is floating down the river and drags it to shore. While he holds the ice in place, the rest of us climb on board. We use the poles to slowly push our way across the water.

Back and forth, back and forth on our icy barge, we ferry the people and supplies to the other side of Sadie Creek. Then my mother helps to drive the four-wheeler onto the ice floe, and we take it over too. Nearly twelve hours after we started our journey, we finally reach the camp.

An ice floe can be a convenient way to cross Sadie Creek. Reggie and his friends use poles to push the raft across the river.

Although there is still a great deal of ice near the shore when the family arrives at Sadie Creek, it is melting every day. In a few weeks, the entire shore will be clear of it.

The camp at Sadie Creek is on the edge of the sea—a good place to view the ice pack. The ice, many miles wide and many miles long, drifts north on offshore currents like a group of floating islands.

Curling inland behind us, the river flows through the frozen arctic plain, called tundra, that stretches farther than the eye can see. The tundra is made up of mosses, lichens, grasses, and many tiny shrubs. There are no large trees, but here and there clumps of small willows rise on the horizon. Plants grow so slowly in the Arctic that a willow as tall as I am might be a hundred years old.

Reggie checks the frame around the window in the sod house to make sure it is tight. The house was made from lumber that washed up on the beach after a storm.

The landscape of gently rolling hills holds many small lakes. The lakes are home to different kinds of ducks and geese. In the marshy places along the shore, my sisters and I hunt for cranberries, salmon-berries, and blueberries.

Our camp has several tents but only one permanent structure. It is a sod house made out of old shiplap lumber. We use the house as a place to sleep since it protects us from the weather. The roof is made of wood with a top layer of sod. This layer of earth cut from the tundra insulates the roof and helps to keep the building warm inside.

The design of our sod house is centuries old. First there is an outer storage room, where we keep our tools, rifles, and supplies. Next comes an inner storage room, where we can hang up our wet clothes to dry. Then comes the largest room, where we all sleep.

This large room has two windows facing the sea. Today the windows are made of glass, but long ago the Inupiat used the stretched and dried stomach of a walrus to keep out the rain and let in the light.

The stove is made from an empty oil barrel that washed up on the beach. Because there are no trees nearby, we use driftwood to fuel the fire for cooking and keeping warm. Our first job is to drive out the ground squirrels that have lived inside over the winter. Then we start a fire in the stove to dry things out.

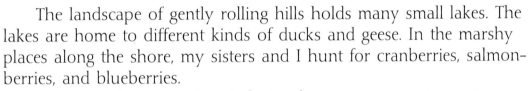

The spongy tundra looks brown in the first weeks after the snow melts each spring, but by summer's end, the landscape will be a brilliant green.

# SETTING THE NET
## KUVRAQTUŁIQ

After setting up camp, my sisters and I watch our father and Aana Vera put the fishnet across Sadie Creek. Vera unfolds the net as my father takes it to the other side of the river in an old rowboat. He attaches it securely to the shore. They make sure that the net is straight and tight. The wooden floats keep it from sinking.

The net has two sizes of holes. Half of them are small, and the other half are large. This way, we are sure to harvest different kinds of fish. Swimming down the river, they cannot see the net and will swim right into it, catching their gills on the string. We like to sit on the shore and watch. We know that when the floats bob up and down, there are fish in the net. At the end of each day, we use a rowboat to collect them.

Vera lets out the net as Reggie's father takes one end to the far shore and fastens it in place.

The fish we catch are called whitefish, northern pike, and arctic char. The fish are scaled, cut, cleaned, and hung out on a rack to dry in the cool air. This is a lot of work, and even the youngest children help.

Later, after the fish have dried, we will pack them in barrels with seal oil to keep them from spoiling. We will eat this dried fish stored in oil over the long winter months. The fish bones are bundled together after they dry. People use the bones as a wintertime dog food.

Sometimes we catch trout in the larger net. We like to eat these fish right away. My mother cooks the trout in a pot over the campfire for dinner. When we have extra fish, we store them in a snowbank, where they will stay cold. The next time someone goes in to Kotzebue, we send fish along for the elders who are too old to go out to camp anymore. We are taught to share what we catch. Sharing is one of our most important Iñupiaq values.

Reggie's father and Vera lift the net out of the water and remove the fish that they have caught. Reggie helps by putting the fish into a gunny sack.

The day's catch goes into a large tub. Reggie's sister Puyuk helps Ross drive the four-wheeler back to camp.

Reggie's sisters Angela and Dawn and his friend Derrick help Aana Vera wash the whitefish.

Vera shows the children how to clean the fish. She uses an ulu (*OO-loo*), or woman's knife, to do the job. The ulu was passed down to her from her grandmother. It is made from an old saw blade and has a handle made of caribou bone. The shape of the handle fits her hand perfectly.

Vera hangs the fish on a wooden rack to dry in the cool air. When the meat is dry, the side with the head and tail will be removed and that part will be used as dog food. The part with the meat will be stored in a cool, dry place or packed in barrels with seal oil. This fish will be eaten during the winter months.

Preparing the fish for drying is traditionally a woman's job, but anyone can learn. Vera shows the children how it is done. She can scale, cut, and clean a fish in just a few minutes. The younger children are encouraged to help with the scaling and washing. Later on, they will learn to use an ulu.

# THE SEAL HUNT
## NIQSAĠNIAŁIQ

For thousands of years our ancestors have relied for their very existence on the animals that live in the sea. Even today, the Inupiat hunt the seals, walrus, and whales of the ocean.

When an animal is killed in the hunt, no part of it is wasted. For example, the meat provides protein in our diet. The fat of these animals, called blubber, flavors and preserves our foods. We make warm clothing from the animal fur, which helps us survive the subfreezing temperatures of the arctic winter. From the animal bones, our people make scraping tools and harpoon heads. We even use the stomach of the bearded seal to make our dance drums!

Every day at the camp, we go out to hunt seals. The men and boys dress in their warmest clothing and set out in a boat toward the ice pack that is slowly moving north, far out at sea. The marine mammals we hunt stay on the ice, and it is there that we must go to find them. Although it might be warm and sunny at camp, the weather out on the ice can be very cold. The wind might blow freezing rain into our faces. A heavy fog could come down and make it hard to see which way to go.

Iñupiaq hunters use binoculars to search the horizon for signs of animal life.

16

I have been following my father and Ross on the hunt since I was five years old. Iñupiaq children are taught about hunting when we are young because there is a lot to learn. The things we need to know cannot be found in books. We gain knowledge by watching and listening, and by trying things out for ourselves.

When hunting for seals, we often travel for hours across the gray waves, searching the ice pack for straight, open leads. These are wide stretches of water, like rivers, between two large sheets of ice. Boats travel on the leads to reach the center of the ice pack.

There we stop the engines and drift silently, watching for signs of the seal and his larger cousin, the ugruk (*OOG-rook*), or bearded seal.

Sometimes we watch and wait for hours. In these quiet moments my father tells me stories of other hunters he has known. His tales describe the dangers they faced and how they survived. The Inupiat have always learned from each other by sharing stories.

Modern boats and rifles are used in the hunt for sea mammals today. Often the boat must be maneuvered through a maze of floating ice. Reggie's father stands on the ice to push the boat through a narrow opening.

Standing up in the boat for a better view of the ice pack, Reggie's father spots some seals in the distance. Although the boat has a gasoline engine, wooden oars are still important. They can be used to push the boat through the ice floes, to propel the boat soundlessly, and as a way to get home if the hunters run out of gas.

On the hunt, my father and Ross have taught me many things about animals and their habits. I know that the best place to find seals and ugruk is near their breathing holes in the ice. Seals can stay underwater for a long time, but eventually they must come up for air. Our ancestors learned that with great patience and skill, they could harpoon the seal at the moment it surfaced.

Another method is to stalk the seal and ugruk as they doze on top of the ice. My father has taught me how to creep across the ice on my belly, using the awkward movements of a seal on land. Sometimes this can fool a seal, since it has poor eyesight. But seals are wary animals, and at the slightest hint of danger, they disappear into the sea.

I have learned about the curiosity of seals. Often they swim up behind our boats when we aren't watching. Perhaps they think we are strange new creatures and want a closer look.

Even though I hunt these animals, I have come to love and respect them. I know that without the seals and the other marine mammals that we hunt for food, our way of life would come to an end.

Ross and my father have taught me about the different qualities of the ice. In the Iñupiaq language, we have many words to describe ice and snow because these conditions are so important to our survival. By its color and texture, I can tell if the ice is thick and strong, or rotting and weak.

I have learned that the ice where we hunt can be very dangerous. A mistake in judgment can cost a person his life. If someone fell into the water, he could freeze to death in a few minutes. There are no Coast Guard boats nearby to rescue people if they run out of gas or get lost in the fog. Here we are entirely on our own. We have only those in our group to rely on for our survival. We learn at a young age to listen to our elders and respect their wisdom in order to stay alive.

Watching Ross and my father, I have learned the proper way to handle a gun. I know how to carry a rifle safely, and I have learned how to shoot it. Although we sometimes use harpoons as our ancestors did, most of our hunting is done with rifles.

While the men and boys hunt, the women and girls wait and watch. They know that when the hunters return, the important work of preparing the meat and hides will begin.

As soon as the animals are unloaded from the boat, Vera, Millie, and my mother will start to remove their hides. Then my sisters will help the women to get the meat ready for drying on the driftwood racks along the beach. Because there is no refrigeration and the sun shines all the time, the women will work without rest until the job is finished.

With his father's supervision, Reggie prepares for a shot. He kneels on the ice to hold the gun steady.

19

While my mother waits, she watches us hunt in her mind's eye. Although we are miles and miles away, she imagines our good luck in the hunt. Sitting on the beach near camp, she waits with my sisters and scans the horizon for signs of our return.

Now that I am ten years old, my parents have given me a hunter's parky. This is a loose-fitting garment with fur on the inside and a white canvas cover on the outside. The parky will help me blend into the horizon of snow and ice and become invisible to the animals I am hunting. On even the coldest day, the ruff of wolverine fur will keep my face warm.

Since coming to camp, we have traveled to the ice many times. We have taken shots at seals and ugruk, but without any luck. Today when we left camp, we took some muktuk (*MUHK-TUHK*) and crackers and a thermos of hot coffee. My father threw a few sleeping bags into the boat and I knew we would stay out on the ice for many hours, perhaps all night. His determined look told me that we would not return to camp until we found some seals to bring back with us.

After six or seven hours of bouncing on the gray waves and staring at the ice, we finally saw a group of ugruk and seals resting near their breathing holes. They weren't too far away, but the men decided to sneak up on them. They wanted to get closer for a better shot. Climbing out on the ice, they crawled toward the seals. I was left with the important job of looking after the boat.

Although I enjoyed watching the men stalk the huge ugruk, I was alert to all the sounds around me. Suddenly I heard the slightest ripple in the water behind the boat. When I looked back, I saw the black eyes of a seal. They popped up just above the waterline a few yards away.

Slowly and carefully I raised the rifle to my shoulder and took aim. I squeezed the trigger, and a shot rang out. In a split second, the seal was mine. Then I threw a harpoon with a float attached into the dead seal's body to keep it from sinking.

Soon I heard two more rifle shots in the distance. My father and Ross returned, dragging a huge ugruk and another seal over the ice. They looked satisfied. But when they came near, I could see the pride in their eyes. They knew that I, too, had killed a seal. I had become an Iñupiaq hunter at last!

Muktuk is a traditional food made from the blubber and skin of either the beluga or bowhead whale, cut up into little squares. A small amount of this food gives the hunters plenty of energy.

Proud to be an Iñupiaq hunter, Reggie stands with his first seal. He wears a traditional hunter's parky and holds a harpoon.

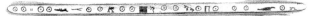

# CAMP CHORES
## IÑUUNIAŁIQ

Using some wooden pegs driven into the ground, Vera stretches the seal hide to dry. Later, in the cold days of winter, she will use the fur to make a pair of boots called mukluks (*MUHK-LUHKS*) for Reggie.

My mother and sisters were very proud of me when I brought the seal back to camp. In our tradition a young hunter shares the first animal he kills with an elder. When a boy gives away his first seal, my people believe that he will have success in the hunt for the rest of his life. It shows that he accepts his responsibility to his family, community, and to the Iñupiaq way of life.

I gave my first seal to our friend Aana Vera. She was honored by the gift and happy because my seal would help to feed her family during the winter. Immediately Vera took the seal and began the job of preparing the meat and hide. Using her ulu, she separated the beautiful spotted fur and the blubber from the body of the seal.

After scraping the thick sheet of blubber from the hide, Vera cut the fat into small cubes and put them into a clean bucket. In a day or two, the oil is rendered from the blubber and can then be used to flavor and preserve many foods. Vera sliced the seal meat into thin strips and hung them on a wooden rack to dry. In the winter months, when Vera shares this meat and oil with her family, she will remember the day when I became a hunter.

Everyone, young and old, helps out with the chores. My mother does most of the cooking over a campfire. The children collect drift-wood, and I help build the fires.

We get our drinking water from a snowbank nearby. My mother calls this our "water pile." She sends my sister to scrape away the top layer of snow and gather clean snow from underneath. After the snow melts, my mother boils the water to make it safe to drink.

Reggie's sister Angela collects a wild herb to make tundra tea.

We put food in a siġluaq (sig-LOG), or arctic icebox, to keep it cold. The icebox is made in the traditional Iñupiaq way, by carefully digging a square hole in the tundra about twelve inches deep. The earth below this level is frozen all year long and is called permafrost. The hole is lined with boards to make a small box and the top is covered with moss and sod for insulation. We keep eggs, bacon, and butter in the icebox so they don't spoil. We can use the siġluaq year after year and never pay an electric bill.

We eat plenty of good food when we are at camp. For breakfast, we like to have bacon and sourdough pancakes. Vera mixes the dough in her tent before she goes to sleep, and by morning it has risen and is ready to cook. For dinner, we have soup made with niġliq (NIG-LICK), or goose, and kurugaq (KOO-roo-guck), which is pintail duck. Sometimes we have a caribou stew or soup made with fresh fish from our net on Sadie Creek.

Reggie's mother cooks the family's meals over a driftwood fire. She always has a pot of water heating for hot chocolate, coffee, or tea.

Because we have such a short growing season, vegetables are hard to find. We enjoy eating sourdock, a wild green plant. We call this quagaq (COH-guck). Another special treat is masu (MAH-soo), a traditional food made from roots preserved in seal oil. Sometimes we find the roots in the burrows of mice that live on the tundra. When we find a cache of roots, we are careful to take only half and to leave the rest. After all, if we are greedy, the poor mouse might starve. Then we wouldn't find any more roots the next year.

# GAMES AT CAMP
## ANIIQSUAŁIQ

When we are at camp, we work a lot but we have fun too. There are endless hours of sunlight, so we are busy all the time. We forget about clocks and calendars. We sleep when we are tired and eat when we are hungry.

We play all sorts of outdoor games. Many of these were invented by our Iñupiaq ancestors and have been played for centuries. They are fun, but they also help us to develop our strength, endurance, and coordination.

One Iñupiaq game is a kind of treasure hunt. Moving slowly along the beach on our hands and knees, we look for a putulik (*POO-too-lik*), a stone that has a hole worn through it. The first person to find one is the winner. When Millie and Vera were girls, they would collect these little stones and thread them into necklaces.

Reggie tries the one-foot high kick with his friend Johnson. Later, the boys try to teach Ross how to play a video game.

Leg wrestling, a search for putiliks on the beach, and snowball fights are all games that Iñupiaq children enjoy.

# CHANGING WAYS
## ATLAĠUQTUQ

Reggie rides a bicycle in front of his house in Kotzebue.

When we go out to camp each spring to hunt and fish, we live a traditional Iñupiaq life. Our time in the wilderness helps us to remember the skills that have allowed our people to survive in this place for so many centuries. It is a chance for us to experiment, to learn, and to enjoy nature.

But when we return to Kotzebue, we go back to a life that is constantly changing. In the old days, our people were isolated from the rest of the world. But now jets land at the airport several times a day, bringing visitors from every corner of the earth. Although our people used to live entirely off the land, today they also have jobs. A paycheck is necessary to buy some of the things we need and want.

My family lives in a modern house with a kitchen, three bedrooms, and a bathroom. Our house is built on stilts to keep it above the frozen ground, and it has every convenience: a telephone, a television, and even a CB radio. We like to eat muktuk and other traditional foods, but we also enjoy pizza, hamburgers, and Chinese food. We shop in a supermarket to buy the fruits and vegetables that we cannot grow in our climate—foods like bananas and watermelon, lettuce and tomatoes.

Reggie's family enjoys pizza at home. In the kitchen, there is a CB radio, which they use to keep in touch with one another. They can talk to someone in the truck or out in a boat. This radio is an important survival tool in the Arctic.

In the wintertime, when the days are dark and cold, we still play outside. Sledding, skiing, and building snow tunnels are fun. But we spend a lot of time indoors too. I like to play basketball with my friends in the school gym, and each year I enter a reading contest sponsored by the schools. Students from all over Alaska compete to see who can remember the most about the books they have read.

Several times a week I go with my sister to practice Iñupiaq dances. Our group performs for people who come from all over the world to visit the Inupiat Cultural Center. All of us who work there are trying hard to preserve the traditional way of life. Although we live in a world of many modern changes, we want to keep the past alive too.

Reggie's sister Angela performs a welcome dance. The fur mittens are a traditional part of her costume. The tassles sewn to the tip of the gloves move as she does. Music for the dances is provided by singers and drummers.

Reggie uses a workbook written in Iñupiaq in this bilingual classroom. In the background next to the computer, handmade dolls are dressed in the traditional fur clothing of the Inupiat.

When my parents were children, there were no schools in their town, so they were sent away from home to attend boarding school in another part of Alaska. With all their classes taught in English, they soon forgot how to speak Iñupiaq, their native language. This has happened to many Inupiat.

But now we are trying to change that. I go to a school near my home where classes are taught in both English and Iñupiaq. We even have textbooks, dictionaries, and workbooks written in our own language.

I know that many of the old ways have been good for our people. The values and traditions of the past have given us the strength and skills necessary to survive in this land. They have made our communities strong and have kept our people together. To re- mind us of these things, our leaders have given us the Inupiat Ilitqusiat (*ee-LIT-koo-sayt*). This is a list of the values that our elders believe are most important to the Iñupiaq way of life. It is a code for us to live by.

# INUPIAT ILITQUSIAT

Every Iñupiaq is responsible to all other Inupiat for the survival of our cultural spirit, and the values and traditions through which it survives.  Through our extended family, we retain, teach, and live our Iñupiaq way.

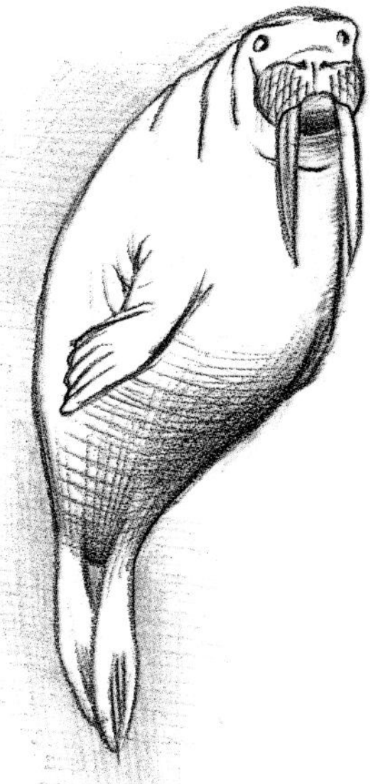

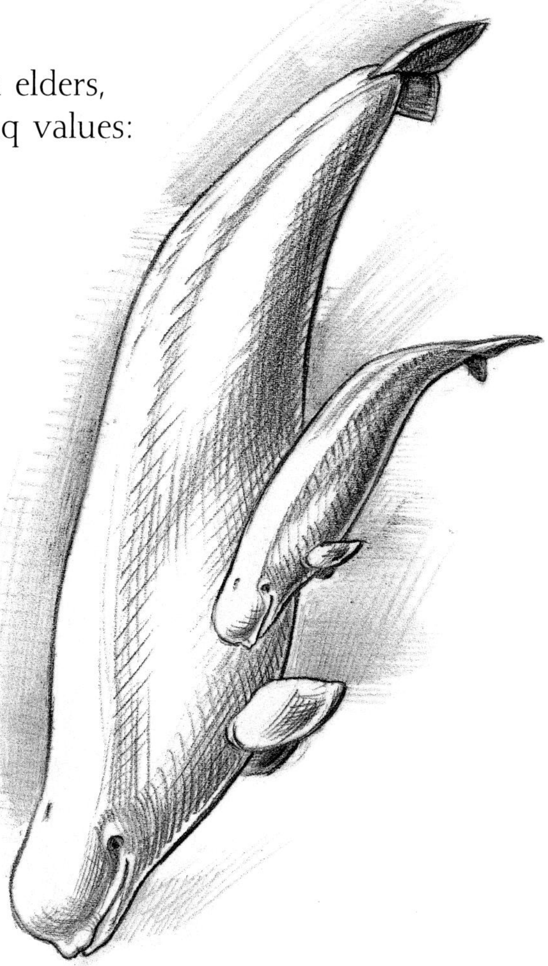

With guidance and support from elders,
we must teach our children Iñupiaq values:

Knowledge of Language

Sharing

Respect for Others

Cooperation

Respect for Elders

Love for Children

Hard Work

Knowledge of Family Tree

Avoidance of Conflict

Respect for Nature

Spirituality

Humor

Family Roles

Hunter Success

Domestic Skills

Humility

Responsibility to Tribe

Our understanding of our Universe and our place in it
is a belief in God and a respect for all His creations.

Flying high in the nalukataq (na-LOO-ka-tak), or blanket toss, Reggie's sister Angela expresses joy in her cultural traditions. Made of walrus hide, the blanket is stretched by the people in the circle to send Angela into the air.

Like our ancestors, the Inupiat today are trying to live in harmony with the earth. We love our way of life—our seasons, the weather, the land, and the animals of the sea and tundra. Although I am only ten years old, I know that I will return each spring to hunt for seals on the ice and take fish from the waters of Sadie Creek. Even though more changes will come, I will continue to live as my parents have taught me—the Iñupiaq way.

# GLOSSARY

**Aana** (*AH-nah*): The Iñupiaq word for "grandmother."

**Aniiqsuałiq** (*an-NEEK-so-lick*): The Iñupiaq word meaning "to be outdoors" or "playing out."

**Arctic:** The region around the North Pole, north of the Arctic Circle.

**Arctic char:** A fish high in fat eaten by the Iñupiaq people.

**Arctic Circle:** The imaginary line circling the North Pole.

**Atlaguqtuq** (*AT-la-GOOK-took*): The Iñupiaq word for "It has changed."

**Aullaałiq** (*oh-LAW-hleek*): The Iñupiaq word that means "going to camp."

**Beluga whale** (*beh-LOO-ga*): A white whale that lives in arctic waters.

**Bering Strait:** A narrow body of water separating North America from the continent of Asia.

**Blubber:** The thick layer of fat found beneath the skin of mammals such as seals, walrus, and whales. Blubber is eaten raw or rendered into oil that is used to flavor and preserve foods.

**Bowhead Whale:** A whale with a huge, arched mouth that lives in arctic waters.

**Cache** (*CASH*): A storage place for food.

**Caribou** (*CARE-i-boo*): A large deer similar to the reindeer that lives on the arctic tundra.

**Chukchi** (*CHUHK-CHEE*) **Sea:** The body of water separating Alaska and Asia north of the Bering Strait.

**Eskimo:** A name for people with similar languages, life-styles, and origins who live in Alaska, Canada, Greenland, and across the Bering Strait in Asia.

**Four-wheel drive:** A vehicle designed for driving in mud or snow that has power on all four wheels.

**Four-wheeler:** A special vehicle for driving in rugged terrain that is the size of a motorcycle but has four large tires with four-wheel drive.

**Gunny sack:** A large burlap sack that can be used to carry heavy items.

**Harpoon:** A pole with a sharp barb on the end used to hunt and retrieve marine mammals.

**Ice floe:** A large sheet of floating ice.

**Ice pack:** Drifting ice floes packed together and carried by ocean currents.

**Ilitqusiat** (*ee-LIT-koo-sayt*): The Iñupiaq word for "their way of being." This is also the title of a code for living created by the Inupiat to preserve their culture and values.

**Iñupiaq** (*in-yoo-PAK*): The language of the Inupiat; anything about or belonging to the Inupiat.

**Inupiat** (*ee-nyoo-PAYT*): The native people who live in the arctic regions of Alaska from Norton Sound north to the Beaufort Sea. The Inupiat speak the Iñupiaq language.

**Iñuuniałiq** (*in-yoo-nyah-LICK*): The Iñupiaq word meaning "activities in order to live."

**Kayak:** A long, narrow canoe, usually for one person, made from canvas, seal, or walrus hides, that is propelled by a paddle with single or double blades.

**Kotzebue** (*COTS-eh-byoo*): A town north of the Arctic Circle on a peninsula that stretches into Kotzebue Sound and the Chukchi Sea. Kotzebue is the center of trade and government for the Inupiat.

**Kurugaq** (*KOO-roo-guck*): The Iñupiaq word for "pintail duck."

**Kuvraqtułiq** (*koov-RAK-too-lick*): The Iñupiaq word that means "to fish using a net".

**Lead** (*LEED*): A channel of water that cuts through floating ice.

**Lichen** (*LY-ken*): A crusty plant formed of fungus and algae that lives on stones, trees, and soil.

**Masu** (*MAH-soo*): The root of the wild Eskimo potato found in mouse caches. Cleaned and preserved in seal oil, it is a food enjoyed by the Inupiat.

**Mukluks** (*MUHK-LUHKS*): Knee-high boots made from seal fur and skin, caribou hides, or wolf fur.

**Muktuk** (*MUHK-TUHK*): A nutritious native food made from the raw skin and blubber of either the beluga or bowhead whale.

**Nalukataq** (*na-LOO-ka-tak*): An Iñupiaq word for the blanket toss, a game in which a person is thrown into the air from a blanket made of walrus hides.

**Niġliq** (*NIG-LICK*): The Iñupiaq word for "goose."

**Niqsaġniałiq** (*NICK-suck-nyah-lick*): The Iñupiaq word for "sea mammal hunting."

**Parky:** A special garment (parka) made of fur, with long sleeves and a hood, used for keeping warm in subfreezing temperatures.

**Permafrost:** A layer of earth below the surface that is always frozen.

**Putulik** (*POO-too-lik*): The Iñupiaq word for a stone or rock that has a hole in it.

**Quagaq** (*COH-guck*): The Iñupiaq word for sourdock, an edible, sweet plant.

**Render:** The process of extracting or removing the oil from blubber.

**Ruff:** A strip of fur around the hood of a parky used to keep the face warm. The best furs, such as wolverine, have hollow hairs that never freeze. This type of ruff will never ice up, even in the coldest weather.

**Shiplap lumber:** Special boards used in boat making. The lower edge of one overlaps the upper edge of the one below.

**Siġluaq** (*sig-LOG*): The Iñupiaq word for an icebox cut into the ground just above the permafrost.

**Sikuliqiruq** (*see-koo-lee-kee-ROOK*): The Iñupiaq word meaning "The ice is breaking up and moving."

**Sod:** A layer of earth with grass growing on it; a piece of the top layer of tundra.

**Tundra:** The frozen arctic plain covered with lichen, mosses, grasses, and dwarf vegetation.

**Ugruk** (*OOG-rook*): A bearded seal.

**Ulu** (*OO-loo*): A cutting tool, also called a "woman's knife," made from a curved saw blade and a bone handle.

# INDEX

Numbers in italics refer to illustrations.

Photo by Tommy Ongtooguk ©1990

The town of Kotzebue is on the tip of a peninsula, surrounded by the sea.

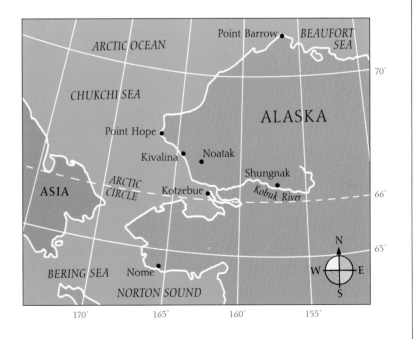

DATE DUE

DISCH.     FEB 0 2 2010

JUL 0 3 2001

DEC 1 5 2002

JAN 0 7 2003

RECEIVED

DEC 1 5 2002

RECEIVED

FEB 0 6 2010